FLOODS
FIRE & FAITH

STORIES OF
FAITH & PERSEVERANCE
IN WORLD DISASTERS

MEMOIRS
Cirencester

Also by Tricia Craib

Amazing Faith: Testimonies of Faith & Perseverance

FLOODS
FIRE & FAITH

STORIES OF
FAITH & PERSEVERANCE
IN WORLD DISASTERS

TRICIA CRAIB

Published by Memoirs

MEMOIRS
PUBLISHING

25 Market Place, Cirencester, Gloucestershire, GL7 2NX

info@memoirsbooks.co.uk www.memoirspublishing.com

Floods, Fire and Faith:
Stories of Faith & Perseverance in World Disasters

All monies accrued from the sales of this book will go to the writing of further Christian stories for children,
for the glory of God.

ISBN: 978-1-909874-46-6

To all children everywhere
who face disasters during their lifetime.

Then Jesus said to them:
"Nation will rise against
nation, and kingdom against
kingdom. There will be great
earthquakes, famines and
pestilences in various places,
and fearful events and great
signs from heaven."

Luke 21:10,11

TABLE OF CONTENTS

FOREWORD

Disasters are a fact of life and can happen suddenly, anywhere and at any time. How we deal with disaster strengthens our character and helps us to cope when another disaster occurs. In these stories six young children survive the particular disaster they face. Some had faith in God, some weren't sure if God really cared about them and one didn't know God at all. Where was God when each disaster struck? He was there right in the middle of it helping and strengthening each child whether they prayed to Him or not. God didn't remove the disaster but helped them through it whether it was an enormous disaster like the Tsunami, Earthquake or the Drought or a smaller one like the Hurricane, Flood or Fire. When we put our trust in God, our faith grows.

These are not real children but they are real disasters. In the stories I have imagined how these children might respond in the face of fear and how each might come to terms with the crisis they experience. Some find courage and maturity in times of struggle while others might find strength in prayer, for God is ever present and cares for us even before we come to know Him.

Tsunami in Sri Lanka

CHAPTER ONE

"**CALL ME** immediately, Prianthe, if you see any sign of the fish," instructed Mohan as he went to the stern of the boat to sort out the fishing net. Prianthe was sitting in the prow of his father's boat looking out at the calm blue sea.

"Don't worry, Father, I can see the fish a mile off," replied Prianthe who was searching the ocean for any sign of the fish. Prianthe had become quite good at recognising the first sign of fish in the water. So good, in fact, that his father had given him the job of "chief fish spotter". He felt very important as he sat staring into the deep blue sea.

While his father was preparing the net Prianthe kept looking for the fish. It was hot in the sun and he began to feel sleepy. He had been up very early that morning to take over from his father who had been on watch all night.

The long hours in the cool of the evening usually brought a good catch of fish but last night there had been nothing. Mohan and Prianthe had cast their net several times but when they pulled it in, not one fish was in the net. They were usually home by breakfast time enjoying some of the fish they had caught before going to the market to sell the rest, but not today. The sellers in the market would be wondering where they were and why they had not come with the fish this morning.

Prianthe looked up from the water and searched the horizon to see if any of the other fishermen were still out at sea. If they had caught some fish they would be at the market by now and would have sold all their catch. No one would want their fish even if they did catch some soon. As he looked all around his boat he noticed several small black dots far away in the distance.

"Ah, the other boats haven't got a catch either, they are still fishing too," Prianthe said to himself. "If we were to find fish now we could be home before them and get a good price for our catch." Prianthe turned his attention back to the sea, examining it carefully, hoping and praying for any signs of the fish.

"See anything?" asked Mohan, when he had finished working on the net.

"Not a thing!" shouted back Prianthe. "I've never seen the sea so quiet. It's so still—nothing seems to be moving down there. The rest of the fishermen are still out at sea too. Look, their boats are out there on the horizon. They must have gone further out to see if there's any fish out in the deep water."

Prianthe's father looked over the edge of the boat, stroking his beard.

"I've never seen the sea so calm at this time of year," he said. "It's quite eerie. I don't like it. I think we will head back."

"But we have no fish to sell at the market," Prianthe replied anxiously. "Mother will not be pleased if we come home without any money. You know she needs to buy things for Arosha's new baby."

"I know, but we have been out all night and caught nothing," replied Mohan. "We have no more water on board. We need to get back. We will try again tonight. I'm too tired to go on fishing. Let's head back to the harbour."

"I wish Jesus was with us today, He would find the fish for us just like in the story you read to us the other night," said Prianthe hopefully.

"Well, I don't know about that," replied Mohan folding away the net. "We can't expect Jesus to wave a magic wand and grant all our wishes. But He does help us when we really need it."

"We really need some fish now," said Prianthe sadly.

"I know," said his father as he began to pull up the sail, "but things don't always happen the way we want them to."

Prianthe leaned over the prow and pulled up the anchor while Mohan set the sail.

CHAPTER TWO

PRIANTHE'S MOTHER Manjula was not very happy when they arrived home with no money and no fish for their meal that night. She decided to send Prianthe and his sister Thilini to see how their sister Arosha was. She lived further up the hillside. Her baby was due very soon and everyone was worried as her husband Gyan, who worked in the city, was not due home for another week.

"But we have no money to give her," Prianthe said, then asked, "Should we not wait till we get some fish tomorrow?"

"No, go now. I'm worried about her being on her own," Manjula replied. "You can stay with her till I come for the delivery of the baby. Gyan has grown some vegetables so there will be something for you to eat."

Prianthe and Thilini began to walk through the village and into the woods at the edge of the hill.

"Why couldn't we all go now?" asked Thilini as they started the long walk to Arosha's village. "What if the baby comes before mother arrives?"

"Don't be silly Thilini; the baby is not due for a week or so. We are just going to see how she is. I can collect some firewood for her and you can pick the vegetables. Come on, we need to hurry! It will soon be dark."

"I'm hungry," complained Thilini.

"So am I. I've been out all night on the boat. I'm tired too but we can't stop here in the woods. Come on, there will be some rice for us at Arosha's," said Prianthe encouragingly.

The two children clambered up the path that led to Arosha's village. Neither spoke as it took all their energy just to climb the hill. Soon they were out of the woods and onto the level area of the hillside where Arosha's village was. The sun was setting over the horizon as they reached Arosha's hut. Arosha was very pleased to see them. They all had some rice then went to sleep.

Early next morning Prianthe got up to look for firewood for his big sister. Many trees grew near the village so the children could gather any fallen sticks. Prianthe knew some of the other boys and arranged to meet them later that morning to climb up to the top of the hill. From there they could look down on the village and the sea in the distance.

Prianthe finished all his chores then told Arosha he was going to find his friends.

"I want to come too," said Thilini. Prianthe didn't want

to take his little sister with him.

"You are too small to climb the hill," he told her. "Besides, you need to stay and look after Arosha. She might need something."

Prianthe hurried off to meet his friends.

"What a view!" exclaimed Prianthe as he reached the top of the hill with his friends. "Look, you can even make out the fishing boats at the edge of the sand."

"Do you see your father's boat?" asked Rohan.

"Yes, I think I can. We live near that bit of rock—see, the one jutting out to the left," replied Prianthe pointing towards the sea. "The men will be getting the boats ready for tonight. Hope they catch some fish this time. We were out all yesterday and caught nothing. It was quite weird; it was so quiet and calm."

The boys lay on the hard ground to rest after the difficult climb to the top. They looked up into the clear blue sky. No birds were flying about. Not a sound was heard as they lay quietly enjoying the heat of the sun and the gentle breeze blowing up the hill from the sea.

Suddenly Rohan sat up. "What's that noise?" he asked as the others jumped to their feet, alarmed at the sudden roaring sound coming from the sea.

"Look, look!" screamed Rohan. "Look at that huge wave

crashing onto the shore! Wow, look at the boats floating up the beach."

"The wave is sucking everything back into the sea!" exclaimed Prianthe as the sea retreated back leaving a huge expanse of sand visible.

The children stood looking at the tiny figures rushing about below them.

"Help, here comes another huge wave," screamed Rohan.

"Oh no, the water is right up over the houses! That was a massive wave!" Prianthe cried holding his hands over his face in horror.

"Look, there's another one coming! Oh no, it's so big it's going to cover your entire village," whispered Rohan.

The boys stood rooted to the spot, staring in complete disbelief as another gigantic wave swept over the land taking everything with it. They were speechless as they watched the disaster unfold below them. They saw people like little black dots running away from the advancing wave before disappearing under a deluge of raging water. They watched as other small dark shapes managed to reach higher ground. After some time the waves retreated back to the sea. The water was calm once more but all along the coast lay a mass of debris, water, and bits of broken boats and houses. They could see dim outlines that looked like bodies floating in the water left behind by the sea. They waited there, unable to move as the real horror of what they had just seen dawned on them.

At last Prianthe whispered, "My parents are down there!"

Rohan put a comforting hand on his shoulder. "Perhaps they managed to get away before the wave struck," he said hopefully.

Prianthe began to run down the hill, crying and shouting, "I need to get back to my village to see if my parents are all right." The other boys followed racing back to their homes. They had to tell everyone about the disaster they had just watched.

Prianthe reached Arosha's home, gasping for breath. His friends shouted to the villagers, "Something awful has happened down at the shore!" No one in the village had seen the waves but they had heard the noise of the waves. Prianthe managed to tell the villagers what they had just witnessed. Several of the men grabbed some ropes and ran down the hill towards the shore. Prianthe and his friends followed them.

As they hurried down the path Prianthe noticed two people climbing up the hill. It was his mother and father.

"What's the matter?" shouted Mohan when they saw the crowd hurrying towards them.

"Didn't you see the huge waves?" asked Prianthe. "We saw it from the top of the hill! Thank God you are safe.

The boats, people, houses – they are all gone!"

"What?" exclaimed Mohan. "We heard the waves breaking onto the shore but we didn't think it was that bad."

"We were worried about Arosha so decided to come and see her," explained their mother. "We left the village about an hour ago and everything was fine then."

"Manjula, you go on to be with Arosha," said Mohan, realising the enormity of what he had just been told. "I will return to our village to see what help we can give. Prianthe, you can come with me."

Mohan and the other men hurried down the hill and through the woods to the stricken village. As they reached the end of the woods they met many of their neighbours running up the hill shouting and screaming. All they could see was water and bodies floating everywhere. There were no houses left standing. The shops, church and school had completely disappeared. Some people were hanging onto the trees while others were clinging to broken bits of wood to keep them afloat.

Mohan and the men rescued as many people as possible. Then they all began to search for any survivors. As the water retreated they tried to salvage what they could from the utter mess that surrounded them.

They buried the bodies, then abandoned what was left of their village. The survivors made their way through the woods to find a safe place to stay for the night, afraid that another tsunami might happen. Prianthe, his father and

some friends went on up the hill to Arosha's village.

They were cold, wet and hungry by the time they reached the safety of Arosha's hut. Thilini came rushing out when she heard voices outside the hut.

"Arosha has had her baby! It's a little boy," she called out to them.

"The baby has arrived already?" asked Prianthe in surprise.

"Yes, yes, come and see. He's beautiful," urged Thilini. Prianthe and Mohan ran into the hut and there was Arosha with a tiny baby in her arms. She smiled at Prianthe and said, "Say hello to your new cousin Gyan. I've named him after his father."

Arosha handed the new born baby to her father. Mohan blessed the baby and looked lovingly at him. Then he handed the baby back to his mother. As he placed the baby in her arms he said, "You know, just as I have placed Gyan into the safe arms of his mother, Jesus places us into the safe arms of God."

As the little family sat round the fire that evening Mohan picked up a Bible and read from it. Then he prayed, "Gracious Heavenly Father, thank you for this new baby we place before you tonight. Bless our little Gyan. Keep him safe in your love. Be with his father as he journeys home. As we thank you for this new life we are mourning the loss of our loved ones. We cannot understand what has happened here today. We don't know what caused the waves to cover and destroy our village. Why Lord, why?" he cried out. The family sat quietly for some time, and then Mohan continued his prayer: "Lord, thank you that we are safe in your loving arms, placed there by Jesus. But where do we start to build up our village again? We have lost everything in the enormous waves."

Mohan could not speak for some time. Then he added, "Lord, we are safe here tonight and we are together. Help us comfort our friends and others who have lost loved ones. Give us strength to start again tomorrow to rebuild our homes and our boats. All we have now is our hope in you, Lord God. Give us your power to cope with what lies ahead. Amen."

Mohan gathered his family together and they hugged each other and cried. This disaster affected them all greatly, but they knew that they would survive and build a future for Gyan and the rest of the children left in their village.

Discussion

1. What Bible story do you think Mohan read to his family that night?

2. Why did some of the villagers not run away when they saw the first big wave?

3. Has anything awful happen to you?

4. How did Prianthe feel when he realised what was happening?

5. I wonder how Arosha felt when her baby was born.

6. Where is God when disasters occur?

7. Who could help when disasters strike?

8. When do we need to pray?

9. How did their faith in God help them?

10. I wonder what you would decide to build first, a home, church or boat.

11. What part of the story did you like best and what part did you not like?

12. Find out about a Tsunami, where they have occurred, and what organisations help with the relief work.

A Disaster at Havasu Village

CHAPTER ONE

ROSEANNE sat on the dusty ground scooping the sand into her blue plastic dish. She watched a boy throwing the sand up into the air. The wind blew the sand

away.

Roseanne joined the boys trying to catch the falling sand. Suddenly the sand disappeared. Roseanne bent down and scraped up another pile of sand into her dish. She was just about to throw the sand up into the air when her mother shouted, "Stop throwing sand about. You will get it in your hair and eyes."

Roseanne dropped the dish of sand onto the ground and ran over to the shop where her mother was standing with lots of bags.

"One day I am going to fly into the sky like the sand," she said looking up into the clear blue sky.
"And how are you going to do that?" asked her mother.

"When I am grown up I am going to learn to fly one of the helicopters that come here," she replied.

"Girls don't fly helicopters," said her brother Pancho who had been standing beside the shop. "It's only the men who have gone to the city to learn how to fly the helicopters that can do that. It's really dangerous."

"Well, I'm going to work hard at school and pass all my exams, and then I will be able to learn to fly a helicopter," said Roseanne.

"Come on," said their mother handing Pancho a big bag of flour. "I have bought all we need for our meal tonight. Let's go home."

"Can I wait till the helicopter comes back?" pleaded Roseanne.

"Yes, but come straight home when it leaves," said her mother, "Pancho can stay with you and bring you home. Don't wait till it comes back again with more supplies. It will be getting dark and I want you home before the sun sets."

"Thanks Mum," shouted Roseanne as she ran off to the field where the helicopter would land.

"Why do I always have to look after Roseanne?" complained Pancho lifting the bag of flour onto his shoulder. "She always wants to watch the men load the campers' backpacks into the helicopter," he grumbled.

"Roseanne is too small to come home by herself," replied his mother. "Look after your little sister and be home before it gets dark."

Roseanne stood by the fence and waited for the helicopter to appear over the rim of the Canyon. She looked up into the cloudless sky. She listened for the familiar humming of the rotor blades. As she waited she climbed onto the fence.

"Get down from there!" shouted a man who was waiting for the helicopter to return.

Roseanne jumped down quickly. She pushed her face against the fence trying to get a better view. She wanted to see everything – the hovering helicopter, the sling swinging down, the men attaching the hook to the sling and, best of all, the big net full of bags being slowly pulled up into the helicopter.

"Don't stand so close or you will get dust in your eyes when the helicopter comes," shouted the man again.

"I close my eyes when the dust rises," Roseanne told the

man. The man came over to where Roseanne was standing. He sat down on the ground beside her.

"I see you here often. Why do you hang about here?" asked the man. "You should be at home playing with your friends."

"I'm going to be a helicopter pilot when I grow up," Roseanne told the man as she sat beside him.

"Girls don't fly helicopters," laughed the man.

"Well, I will be the first girl from our tribe to fly one," replied Roseanne confidently.

"Listen, I can hear the helicopter coming," said the man getting to his feet. "Remember, stay away from the helicopter. It's not safe for children to be around here. If you get hit by the blades you will not be flying anything."

Roseanne stood behind the fence. She looked up into the sky and saw the helicopter in the distance. Pancho wandered over to where Roseanne was standing. She jumped up and down shouting excitedly, "Here it comes. Look, Pancho the helicopter is coming!"

Soon the sound of the turning blades filled the air and the dust began to blow about as the helicopter landed right in front of Roseanne. When the dust settled Roseanne noticed some men coming out of the helicopter.

As soon as the men were safely behind the fence the helicopter rose into the air once more. The man who had shouted at Roseanne ran to the net which was full of the backpackers' bags. He quickly hooked the net on to the rope which was dangling from the hovering helicopter. He waved to the pilot and the helicopter swung round and headed off back up to the rim of the Canyon.

"One day I will go up to Halapai Hilltop," Roseanne told Pancho.

Roseanne's family lived about a mile from the village. Her parents looked after the camp site used by visitors to the Havasu Falls. There were always lots of people from different countries camping by the side of the river. Roseanne enjoyed watching them and listening to the different languages they spoke.

"Come on Roseanne," said Pancho lifting the bag of flour onto his shoulder. "We need to go home now."

When they returned home Roseanne told her family all about what she had seen.

"I'm going to fly the helicopter up to the rim and back to our village with food and luggage," she told her father as they all sat down to eat.

"Well, you will need to work hard and do all your school work, then you can go to the college in the city," said her father patting her on the shoulder. "Then one day you just might be able to learn to fly a helicopter."

"Don't be silly," said Pancho, "Roseanne will never be able to fly a helicopter. She's a girl and much too small."

"I'm not too small. I will grow soon," said Roseanne as tears filled her eyes.

"There's no harm in aiming high," said her mother kindly. "If you boys would work as hard and pay attention to your teachers instead of fooling around all day, you might get a good job too."

"What's the point?" asked Pancho angrily. "We will never get good jobs. School is a waste of time." Pancho slammed down his spoon and went outside.

"Come back and finish your meal," shouted his mother, but Pancho ran off to find his friends.

"Why is Pancho so angry all the time?" asked Roseanne sadly. "He doesn't go to school and he is always being nasty to me."

"Oh, that is just what boys do as they grow up," said her mother clearing away his plate. "Now you eat up and don't worry about Pancho. He will go back to school next term. I just wish he had great ideas like you Roseanne."

"I can hear the helicopter," shouted Roseanne jumping up from the table and running out of the door. She stood on the path watching the helicopter fly over her house on its way back up to the rim of the Canyon.

Later that evening Pancho returned with the news that a flash flood was expected.

"The water in the river has turned a reddish brown and the tribal officer is telling the campers to be on the lookout for the river rising," Pancho gasped excitedly.

"I noticed the thunder clouds in the distance over by the dam as I came home tonight," said their father. "But there was no warning report sent out."

Just then a light flashed on the two way radio lying on the table.

"That will be a message for me," said their father picking up the radio and going out the door. Roseanne watched her father pacing up and down outside their house talking on his radio. When he had finished talking he came into the house and collected his torch and some rope.

"I've been called out on duty tonight," he said. "We've been notified by the National Weather Service that the water levels up at Havasupai Creek are rising. I have to go and warn the campers to pack up and head for higher ground. I just hope the dam is holding back the water. We don't want any accidents."

"Can I come with you?" asked Pancho who suddenly became interested in the campers.

"Yes, you can walk up the creek and let everyone know to get to higher ground just in case," replied his father as he went out of the house.

"Do you think anything will happen to us tonight?" asked Roseanne a little afraid.

"No, don't you worry," said her mother quietly. "Everything will be all right. We haven't had a flood here for over thirty years, so warning the campers is just a precaution in case the river level rises. Now off you go to bed and sleep well."

That night as Roseanne lay on her bed she thought

about the helicopter, and the campers who visit their famous Falls. She thought about the pilots who flew the helicopters bringing people and supplies from the rim of the Canyon.

"I'll need to be very clever to fly a helicopter," Roseanne thought to herself as she fell asleep.

CHAPTER TWO

"**WAKE UP ROSEANNE**, wake up. We need to leave the house right away!" shouted her mother as she tried to wake Roseanne.

Roseanne opened her eyes and sat up. "What's wrong?" she asked sleepily.

"Quick, we need to go! The dam has overflowed and the river is flooding!" said her mother in alarm, handing Roseanne her dress and sandals.

Roseanne was very frightened. She dressed quickly and followed her mother out of the house. It was raining and dark outside. She felt her mother take her by the hand and before she could think about what was happening they were running along the muddy path to the village. She was out of breath and had lost her sandals but she knew she had to keep running. Roseanne wondered what was going on as she saw many others running along the path too. Soon they came to the trees beside the river. Roseanne could hear the water thundering down.

"Your father told me some of the bridges have been

washed away," explained her mother as they ran through the cottonwoods. "We needed to go back to the village, so keep running Roseanne; we have no time to spare."
Suddenly there was a terrible crashing noise as a nearby tree was swept away by the rushing water.

"What was that?" Roseanne asked breathlessly.

"The power of the water coming over the waterfall is so strong it has pushed the tree over," her mother managed to shout over the noise. "Just keep going Roseanne; we need to get to the helicopter pad. The ground is higher there and hopefully they will come and rescue us."

Roseanne notice more shapes in front of her now. Other people from the campsite were trying to reach safety too. Some were dressed in only shorts and sleeveless tee-shirts. Everyone was running away from the water which was cascading down the river bed and flowing onto the path. Roseanne tried to keep up with the others but it was hard for her to run through the mud on the path. Her feet kept slipping and several times she had to grab onto her mother's skirt or she would have fallen in the mud. Suddenly there was no path, only water.

"The river has burst onto the path!" shouted one of the men. "This whole area is flooded. We can't get to the village this way. We will need to go back."

"We can't go back!" screamed another man. "Look, the water is rising behind us. We are trapped!"

"Wait here Roseanne. I'll see how deep it is," said her mother pulling up her skirt and wading knee deep into the water. "I'll send someone to get you," she called back as she went deeper into the water. Roseanne watched her mother as the water reached above her waist. Other people had also followed her into the water. Some were struggling through the flooded area in the hope of reaching the village and higher ground. Roseanne began to cry when suddenly she couldn't see her mother. Lots of noises could be heard – people screaming, branches breaking and water roaring. Roseanne felt the ground below her feet vibrate. She saw someone come towards her out of the water; then she felt herself being lifted off the ground by strong arms and carried through the water.

"Don't worry 'little helicopter pilot'," I will get you safely through this flood." It was the man from the helicopter pad. Before she knew it Roseanne was safely through the freezing water. There, at the edge of the flood, stood her mother dripping wet. Lots of people were standing shivering on this small bit of ground that was above the rising water. Horses were running wildly about through the crowds, obviously afraid too. An old woman was handing out blankets to the freezing people.

"Here, take the child's wet clothes off and wrap her in this blanket," the old woman told Roseanne's mother. It was difficult to remove the soaking dress but carefully her mother managed to get Roseanne out of the cold, wet dress and wrapped her in the coarse dry blanket.

Suddenly Roseanne heard the familiar sound of the helicopter.

"The helicopter is coming to rescue us," her mother whispered.

"Yes, you will get your trip in the helicopter tonight," said the man. "I will make sure you get to ride up beside the pilot."

Roseanne stood shivering, holding the blanket round her, waiting for the helicopter to arrive. As the light from the helicopter shone out of the darkness, she noticed the mighty surge of foaming water roaring past them. One wrong move and she knew she would be in that awful water. Now she was really scared. All her young life she had wanted to ride in the helicopter but now it looked very dangerous and scary as it couldn't land on this small bit of dry ground. The only way to be rescued was to hold onto the rope dangling from the helicopter and be swung up into it. Roseanne remembered what her brother had said about it being too dangerous for girls to do this job. Perhaps he was right after all.

"Where is Pancho?" she asked her mother, suddenly realising she had not seen him.

"I don't know, I just hope he is safe somewhere," said her mother looking round the crowd of campers and villagers.

"Children and mothers with babies first," said the man from the helicopter pad.

When it was Roseanne's turn to get into the helicopter she clung to her mother afraid to let her go.

"I will take her up with me," the man told Roseanne's mother. Turning to Roseanne he said kindly, "Come with me. You will meet up with your mother again at Halapai."

The man grabbed the rope that was hanging from the helicopter, then lifted Roseanne with his other arm and held her tightly. Together they swung slowly up into the helicopter.

"Hold on tight," he told Roseanne. "By the way, my name is Mike."

"My name is Roseanne," she managed to shout back as

they swung up to the open door of the hovering helicopter. Once inside he lifted her into the front seat of the helicopter and fastened the seatbelt. As he was about to leave Roseanne pulled at his shirt sleeve.

"Mike, will you look for my brother Pancho?" she shouted.

"Don't worry, I will find him. I have to go and help the others. The pilot will take care of you," he said. Then, turning to the pilot, Mike said, "This young lady wants to be a helicopter pilot when she grows up."

The pilot patted her on the leg and gave her the thumbs up sign. When all the seats inside the helicopter had been filled, the pilot hoisted up the rope. Finally they were flying away from the raging river. As Roseanne looked out of the window, she realised she didn't feel scared any more. She watched the sky turn a pale pink as the sun began to rise over the rim of the Canyon. As they approached the rim Roseanne could see that there were lots of people there. The noise of the helicopter meant that the pilot didn't hear Roseanne thanking him.

Before she knew it the helicopter was back on the ground. Her trip in the sky was over. The pilot unfastened the seatbelt and someone lifted her out of the helicopter. Another stranger carried her to a waiting van. As they went into the van she heard the helicopter take off again.

"Your mother will find you at the Red Cross Shelter at

Peach Springs," said the stranger who was carrying her. "We need to take you there to make sure you are okay. Don't be afraid, this nurse will look after you."

The nurse took Roseanne and wrapped warm blankets round her. Then she strapped her into the seat and gave her some water to drink. Several other people were already in the waiting van. Roseanne looked out of the door before the helpful stranger closed it. She saw the helicopter swoop over the rim going back down for more of the stranded people. Suddenly Roseanne felt very cold and tired but she was glad of the soft, warm blankets round her.

At the special shelter set up for the survivors Roseanne was given warm dry clothes, some food and a warm drink. She was shown to a small mattress on the floor and told to rest till her mother arrived. Roseanne closed her eyes knowing that her parents would come to get her as soon as they were rescued from the flood.

The following day a very relieved Roseanne saw her mother coming into the centre.

"We have to stay here for a while until we get word that it is safe to go home," her mother told her.

"Where are Father and Pancho?" asked Roseanne.

"We don't know where Pancho is, but your father is safe," said her mother sadly. "Your father searched for him all night but no one has seen him. Father has stayed at the village to look for him and help the campers get out safely. Hopefully when Pancho is found they will return home to sort out the damage to our house."

"Mike will find Pancho," said Roseanne confidently. "He promised to find him, so don't worry Mother, I'm sure he will be all right."

"Yes, I know he will be found,' replied her mother. "Everyone is looking for him."

"When can we go home?" Roseanne asked one of the helpers who brought them some food.

"Not until the water has gone down again," said the helper. "Then it will be safe for you to return to your home or what is left of it after the flood."

Roseanne's mother warned her, "Our home may not be the same when we get back. The flooded river caused a lot of damage."

"We will arrange for you to go home by helicopter as soon as we hear it is safe to do so," said the helper. "You would like that Roseanne wouldn't you?"

Roseanne didn't mind staying at the centre. The aid workers were very kind and they got lots of good food. The thought of going home in the helicopter excited her too. A few days later a nurse came in.

"There's someone here to see you," said the nurse.

Roseanne looked up and couldn't believe her eyes. Standing by the door was the pilot with his earphones still on his head and his big gloves in his hand.

"'I've come to take you home in the helicopter," he said. "The water has gone down and your house has been repaired. It's safe now for you to go home. Your father is waiting for you at the helicopter pad."

A group of people joined Roseanne and her mother in the van which took them from Peach Springs to Halapai Hilltop. There the helicopter was waiting for them. Inside the helicopter Roseanne got another surprise. Mike from the village was waiting for her.

"Did you find Pancho?" she gasped as she rushed up to Mike.

"Yes, we found him but I will let Pancho tell you all about it," said Mike showing Roseanne to the front of the cockpit. When she was sitting down he fastened her seatbelt.

"Now you can see how a pilot flies the helicopter," said Mike. The pilot jumped up into the front seat beside Roseanne. He showed Roseanne everything in the cockpit and explained what the dials were for. He showed her the peddles and even let her move the throttle to make the helicopter rise into the air. Roseanne was so excited! This trip home made her quite sure she really did want to learn to be a helicopter pilot when she was old enough.

As they neared the village landing area Roseanne could see her father and Pancho standing on the ground below.

She waved to them as the helicopter circled the field. When they landed, Pancho ran to meet them. He shook Mike's hand, "Thank you for coming back to get me. I thought I would never be found up that tree. I was so scared; no one knew where I was. So thanks again, Mike."

"Don't thank me," said Mike. "It was your little sister here who asked me to find you. She's the one to thank."

Pancho gave Roseanne a big hug. "Thank you for noticing I was not with you," he said. "Thank you for caring about me so much that you asked Mike to look for me. If it wasn't for you I might have been swept away by the floods. Mike found me hanging onto a tree and guided the helicopter to rescue me."

As the little family walked back home Pancho said, "I hope you will become a helicopter pilot when you grow up, Roseanne. They do a wonderful job and are very brave. It takes a lot of skill to bring a helicopter down at the right spot. Perhaps I will be one too."

"Well," said his father, "you will need to go to school and listen to the teachers."

"Yes Father, I'll be going back to school and I'll work hard. I've learned my lesson and I won't be fooling about as I was doing. I will be like Roseanne here and have an ambition to be someone good and helpful when I grow up."

On the way back to their home Roseanne asked Pancho all about his adventure.

"Well," began Pancho, "I was hurrying along the path by the river, warning the campers to pack up and move to higher ground as Father had told me, when this mighty roar of water came rushing down. It happened so quickly everyone was caught in the raging water. I somehow managed to grab hold of a branch of a tree and climb up the tree trunk. I held on tightly to the tree trunk. The water rose quickly and soon it was over my waist. The swirling water kept pushing my legs away. My arms were getting tired. I didn't know how long I could hold on. I could see other campers in the trees beside me calling to their friends. It was very scary. I thought I was going to be pulled into the water and drowned."

"What happened next?" asked Roseanne in amazement.

"Just as I was about to let go, I heard Mike calling my name. I shouted to him. He had a torch and shone it through the trees. He saw me clinging to this thin ash tree. He waded into the raging water, grabbed hold of me and helped me down. Then he led me to the higher ground. He went back into the water several times to help others. When the helicopter hovered above us he shone his torch so that the pilot could see us. They let down the rope and Mike grabbed it. He fastened it round my waist and I was pulled up into the helicopter."

"You certainly had quite an experience," said his mother as they arrived at their house. Roseanne stopped and looked at the mess that lay in front of her. Debris and mud covered the ground. A fallen tree lay across the path. All their plants and vegetables had been washed away.

"What a mess!" was all she could say.

"Don't worry, we will soon have it cleared up," said her father brightly.

The family went inside their house. The broken window panes were boarded up making it dark inside. As the children sat round the table waiting for something to eat, they discussed the events of the last few days.

"I was so scared that I even prayed to God to help me," whispered Pancho to Roseanne. "I believe in God now after being saved from the flood."

"I was praying too," whispered Roseanne. "I knew He would help us. I'm glad you believe now too."

That night the family thanked God for saving everyone from the raging water and bringing them safely together again. Pancho told his parents that he would go with them to the little Bible Church in the village. He offered to say the prayer thanking God for the food they were about to eat. After their meal Pancho helped his father clear the fallen tree away while Roseanne helped wash up the dishes.

"Maybe we could have our own rescue helicopter," laughed Roseanne as they lay in their beds that night. "We could find and help people. I would be the pilot, and you could go down on the rope to save the people."

Everyone laughed, happy to be safe after the ordeal of the flash flood caused by the breaching of the Redlands Dam—a flood that, in a matter of hours, took the calm, smooth flowing, blue-green river to a record breaking eight feet above the normal water level.

The river would revert to its former glory. The pathways would be restored once more. The hikers would soon return to enjoy the beautiful waterfalls, to swim in the still pools and camp among the lush green vegetation of the ash and cottonwood trees.

Discussion

1. What part of the story did you like best?

2. Do you think the hikers returned to Havasu Falls?

3. Would they be afraid that the river might flood again?

4. What do you want to be when you grow up?

5. When has someone been unkind to you?

6. Which of the characters in the story would you like to be?

7. Why do you think Pancho was always angry and unhappy?

8. I wonder what the river was like when the dam overflowed.

9. Who can you help when they are in need?

10. How do floods happen?

11. Who or what organisations help when there is a flood disaster?

12. Where is Havasu? Find out about the people who live there.

An Earthquake in Pakistan

KIMAYA opened her eyes but she could see nothing. She tried to move her legs but nothing happened. Gently she lifted her head and turned it to the side. She still couldn't see anything. Lifting one hand carefully she felt above her head and beside her body. All she could feel were the hard bits of rubble all around her and some soft earth underneath her head. She tried to lift her other hand but it wouldn't move. She realised her body ached as she lay quite still listening for any sound that might help her understand what had just happened. All she could hear was silence. Kimaya heard no sound of voices, no noise of the trucks on the road, no birds singing. Suddenly she heard the sound of falling rain above her head. It was soft and intermittent at first but soon the noise became louder and more persistent. She thought she could also hear a sound like the howling of the wind every now and again. Did that rumbling noise wake her from sleep only minutes before? Where were her brothers and sister who were sleeping nearby? She called quietly in the darkness, "Sahar, are you there? Rana, Bahir, are you all right?" There was no reply, no movement, and no sound to tell her anyone was near.

It had all happened so quickly - the rumbling noise, her bed shaking, the sound of crashing timber and then nothing. Kimaya thought she remembered falling and hurting her head. She remembered the dust and noise, then the silence. She tried to move her legs again but they seemed to be trapped by something heavy. Then she realised she couldn't feel her legs, couldn't wriggle her toes or move her feet. She couldn't sit up as her head hit something when she tried. Her head was now throbbing and she became aware of the pain in her chest.

"Breathe slowly," she told herself, trying to keep calm. Now she was beginning to feel scared. It was difficult to breathe. She was afraid of the darkness, afraid of the loneliness. She wondered where she was. What had happened? Why was no one else here? Her home had been full of friends and family.

As she lay still in the darkness Kimaya began to cry. Tears trickled down her cheeks and her nose became blocked up, making her breathe through her mouth. Her throat felt dry as she sobbed quietly. Her eyes closed again as she gave way to sleep.

Kimaya woke with a start. She was aware of a lot of noise going on above her head. The rain was falling on something hard now, making a strange pitter-patter sound. She could hear voices shouting and hammers banging all around her. Her heart began to beat quickly. She felt about her but there were no signs that anything had changed in her small dark hole. Again she tried to move her legs but nothing happened. She called out, hoping someone would hear her, but the noise above smothered her tiny voice. By now she was feeling very tired and thirsty. Her head still hurt and her voice was very quiet. She wanted to close her eyes again but somehow she knew she must stay awake. She had to let whoever was making all that noise know she was still alive.

Kimaya waited quietly, listening carefully for any lull in the noise above. As she listened she could make out the voices of men and women, the roar of engines going backwards and forwards and the incessant hammering. Then all was quiet. She tried to call out but her voice was just a whisper. Then she felt around her to find something hard to bang against the roof of her prison. When she eventually found a piece of rock, she realised that the noise had started again.

"Hopefully they will stop soon," she told herself. "Then I can bang on the roof with this rock." Feeling carefully above her, she tried to reach the place where she had bumped her head. Once she had found the hard place she tried banging on it. Her arm soon became tired, so she decided to rest till it was quiet again. Her eyes kept closing so she tried to think of a way to keep herself awake. She remembered the happy songs she had learned at the Mission School. So she kept singing the words in her head till she noticed it was quiet again. Quickly, she picked up the bit of rock and once again began banging on the roof. The noise started again. They had not heard her.

Kimaya tried not to cry. It was hard enough to breathe in this tiny space without blocking up her nose as well. She sniffed back her tears and waited for the noise to stop. While she waited she thought about the stories of Jesus she had heard about.

"Perhaps Jesus will help me," she thought.

When she had sung all the songs she knew and thought about all the stories she could remember, she decided to listen for the different noises she could hear. What was going on out there? Who was hammering above her? Was it her father? Kimaya knew that he would certainly be pulling away any rubble to get to his beloved family if he knew they were trapped down here. The thought of her father brought stinging tears to her eyes again.

"Perhaps he is down here too," she thought. "He may be trapped or even dead." That thought sent shivers down her back and she began to panic. She tried not to think about it. Quickly she said another prayer asking God to help the people to find her. Then she listened again. There were other voices talking now. These voices were speaking in a different language.

"They must be rescuers from another village," she thought, "or maybe from another country." This gave her fresh hope and she felt for her rock ready to bang again when the noises above stopped.

Time seemed endless as Kimaya waited. Every time the

noise stopped she banged as hard as she could on the roof, but nothing happened. The constant banging caused bits of rubble to fall on her face. She knew she was in a very dangerous situation. One wrong move and everything could fall in on top of her. She was very scared. Now she knew that she could be buried under all the debris.

"I wonder how long I have been down here," she thought. She was getting so tired she could hardly lift the rock. She felt so helpless, alone and afraid in this dark, dirty hollow. She was stiff and sore and her throat burned. All she wanted to do was go to sleep again. Then it would all be over. If she shut her eyes soon the pain would go away. She wouldn't notice the darkness. She could dream about her family and friends. Just as she was about to close her eyes for the last time the noise stopped and a voice shouted: "Is anyone there? Can you hear us?"

"Don't give up," shouted another voice. "We are searching for you, Kimaya. Nearly all the rubble has been removed. Make some noise to let us know you are still alive."

Kimaya recognised her father's voice! Somehow she managed to grab the rock and with one last effort she hit the roof above her head.

"She's still alive. Praise God!" she heard her father shout. He had come to save her. Somehow he had known she was there. He had called her by name. Now she must hold on. She wasn't going to die after all. Her rescuers were near and they would soon have her out of this awful place. Tears ran down her face and into her open mouth. She tasted the saltiness on her lips. She smelt the dust all about her, but she could feel nothing. Her body was cold and lifeless, and her eyes closed slowly.

"I've got her, I've got her!" shouted the rescuer, who was lying flat on his stomach reaching into the wreckage of what had once been a beautiful house. Concrete, wood, glass and earth were strewn all about him. A rain soaked arm had found the tiny, frozen body.

"I can't move her," he called over to the other rescuers. "Her legs must be caught under some rubble." Turning towards the small opening in amongst the debris, he called out, "Hold on Kimaya, I'll get you out as quickly as I can. Your father is here beside me."

Kimaya didn't understand what the man was saying. She didn't know what language he was speaking but she knew he would pull her out of this disaster.

"The rescuers are just removing a large bit of concrete which is on top of your legs," Kimaya's father told her. "Then the rescuer will pull you free. Can you reach up for his hand?"

Kimaya opened her eyes. For the first time she saw some light streaming through a small gap in the rubble above her. She felt the sudden rush of cold air filling her tiny space.

Through this hole she also saw the hand of her rescuer, but she felt nothing. Somehow she managed to move her hand to reach up and touch his hand.

"She's moving!" the man called out. "I've got hold of her hand. Quick, lift that bit of concrete away. If we can free her legs I can pull her out."

The next thing Kimaya knew was being wrapped up in a blanket and carried by her father. He was running towards a large black helicopter which was waiting on the ground surrounded by army officers.

"Thank God you're safe," whispered her father.

Kimaya felt the cold, refreshing rain lash her face. She could make out two helicopters in the dark sky above and heard the deafening hum of the helicopter rotors.

"Angels have come to save us!" she thought as her father hurried on through the pouring rain. She heard people screaming and shouting. Then Kimaya felt herself being handed to another person and placed on the floor of the helicopter beside other injured people. As the engines roared she felt the helicopter rise off the ground.

"You're safe now," shouted her father as he waved to the departing helicopter. "They will take you to the hospital. I will meet you there later. Don't be afraid, they will take care of ...." Her father's voice got lost in the noise from the helicopter.

Kimaya opened her eyes and tried to speak to her rescuers but no words came. She gave a brief smile, closed her eyes and waited. There was nothing left for her to do now but to thank God for answering her prayers. She had been saved. She was still alive, and would soon be well again.
Kimaya had been rescued from her prison under the rubble caused by the earthquake!

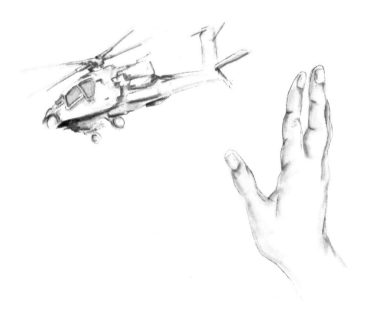

Discussion

1. What part of the story did you like the best?

2. What part did you not like? Why?

3. Can you imagine what it would be like buried under all that rubble?

4. I wonder how Kimaya's father felt when he realised his daughter was trapped.

5. When have you been afraid or in a frightening situation?

6. Who helped you?

7. Have you prayed to God for help?

8. Where is God when disasters happen?

9. Why do you think earthquakes occur?

10. How did Kimaya survive the earthquake?

11. Where is Pakistan?

12. Find out who, along with the Pakistan army helicopters, helped, such as doctors and aid workers.

A Drought in Laos

CHAPTER ONE

"**D**ON'T WASTE THE WATER!**"** shouted Vorn's mother from the house. Vorn had been filling her tin with water from the outside tap. She looked at her mother and said, "I'm not wasting the water, Mother, I'm giving my papaya tree a drink. It's dry and needs some water."

"We need the water too," replied her mother harshly. Vorn looked at the water in her tin. She didn't know what to do with it. Should she water her tree or take it to her mother?

"Can I just give my tree one last drink?" she called to her mother. "The tree will die if I don't give it some water."

"All right," said her mother, "but don't spill any of it. We've not had any rain for several months and if it doesn't rain soon no one will have any water to drink."

Vorn carefully carried the tin full of water to where her

little tree was growing. She poured the water gently round the roots and watched as the water disappeared into the ground.

"There, that should keep you going for another day," she told the tree. Vorn covered the earth with some stones to keep the sun from drying up the water. She sat looking at her tree.

"I don't know what I will do if there is no rain soon. Mother won't let me take any more water from the tap. I don't want you to die after all the care I have taken over you," she told the tree. Vorn was sad that the rains had not come as expected. They no longer had to wash each night after school and there was not enough water to wash their clothes either. Vorn broke a large leafy branch off a nearby tree and laid it against her papaya.

"That will give you some shade from the sun," she said.

"Who are you talking to?" asked Taan, Vorn's brother. He was on his way home from the rice fields when he saw Vorn talking to herself.

"I'm talking to my tree," answered Vorn.

"Talking to a tree?" Taan asked in surprise. "I didn't know trees had ears," he said, laughing at her.

"Of course they don't have ears, silly," said Vorn, and she began to laugh too.

"Then why are you talking to a tree?" asked Taan.

"It's my papaya tree that I got from Uncle Ponsee," Vorn said. "It should produce fruit soon, then we can enjoy eating papayas. The problem is the rains haven't come and we mustn't waste the water. Mother said I was not to give it any more water. I don't want it to die, Taan. Uncle Ponsee said he wanted to see a really big tree the next time he came to visit us," Vorn explained sadly.

"I don't know why you are bothering about a silly little tree. How do you know it will grow fruit? You are wasting time and effort looking after it," said Taan crossly as he began to walk away.

"I'm sure it is a fruit tree," answered Vorn. "Uncle Ponsee said it would grow lots of papayas."

"But that is the problem," explained Taan. "You don't know if it is a good tree till it is big and fruit appears."

"Well, I want to look after it whether it is a good tree or not. I am going to take care of it and it needs water," said Vorn stubbornly, following her brother back to their house.

"It has water now," said Taan. "Perhaps the rain will come soon. Come on, it must be time to eat. I'm hungry."

Just as Vorn was going into the house she suddenly remembered her tin. She ran back to the tree, picked up her tin and returned to the house.

CHAPTER TWO

"**T**HERE'S NO WATER** coming out of the tap!" shouted Taan several days later. Their father came running out of the house and looked at the tap. Sure enough, there was no water coming out of it at all.

"I was afraid this would happen," said their father. "We will just have to go to the spring up in the hills. We used to get our water from there before they piped the water to the taps outside each house in the village."

"Where is the spring?" asked Vorn excitedly. The thought of no water in the tap had made her very sad as she knew that her tree would not last another day without water.

"Oh, it's quite far away," said Taan. "You are too small to get up there, but don't worry, we will go and fetch some water from the spring."

Vorn watched them leave. Many other people from the village were on their way to the spring with buckets, tins and jars—anything that would hold some water.

"You stay here and take care of the baby," said Vorn's mother as she too followed the others to get some water.

It was very hot and the baby was asleep inside the house. Vorn went to sit outside in the shade of the house near the tap. Suddenly she felt a drip of water fall from the tap onto her arm. She jumped up quickly, wiping the drop of water from her arm. She looked at the tap. Then she turned on the tap. No water came from it. She felt under the tap but it was dry. Vorn sat back down again. She started to sing to herself while she waited for her family to return with the water. Then she heard another drip from the tap and saw a wet mark on the ground. She stood up again and watched the tap. After several minutes the tap let another drip fall.

Vorn rushed inside the house and found her tin. Carefully she placed it under the tap and waited. Eventually one drip hit the bottom of the tin with a quiet *plop*.

"If I leave my tin there all day and all night I might just have enough water to give to my tree," she said to herself. She knew there would be no spare water for her tree, but she hoped that there might just be enough water dripping from the tap to keep her tree alive. She sat and watched the drips splashing into her tin.

Then she heard the baby cry. She got up and went to take care of him. Soon the others arrived back with water from the spring in the hills. The women began to prepare the evening meal and boil the rice.

CHAPTER THREE

"**W**HAT have you got there?" asked Mother the next day when she saw Vorn holding her tin.

"I have collected some water from the dripping tap," she answered happily. "Look Mother, there is just enough water to give my tree a little drink." Her mother looked into the tin and sure enough, there was a little drop of water at the bottom of the tin. She watched as Vorn carefully carried it to her tree and poured it onto the roots. She noticed how Vorn gently put the stones back over the damp earth.

"I wish we had enough water to give some to your little plant," said her mother as Vorn came back into the house.

"Can I go with Taan tomorrow to get some water from the spring?" pleaded Vorn.

"If he will take you, but remember you will have to walk all the way," replied her mother.

"Oh, I will walk all the way. I'm strong and my tree needs some water," said Vorn excitedly.

Just then a neighbour came up to Vorn. She was carrying a bit of Lao skirt fabric known as a sin.

"Put this round your tree, Vorn. It might help to make the tree produce some fruit," she said, holding out the sin.

"Thank you," said Vorn taking the sin. Vorn looked at her tree and wondered how the sin wrapped round a tree could make it have fruit.

She ran into the house with the sin and asked her mother, "Does putting a sin round a tree make it grow fruit?"

Her mother thought for a while, then said, "Some people think it does, but others say it is just an old wives' tale."

Before Vorn could decide if she should put the sin round the tree, Taan came back from the fields where he had been working.

"Can I come with you to the spring for some water?" asked Vorn hopefully. "My papaya tree needs some."

"You can come with me if you promise to walk all the way," Taan said, adding, "I am not carrying you, Vorn."

Vorn dropped the sin on the ground and ran to get her tin.

Taan took Vorn to the hills where the spring was. It was hard for Vorn to keep up with her brother as she needed to stop every now and then. Eventually they reached the spring but Vorn had to sit down and rest before she could collect her water. Taan waited patiently for his little sister. After they had collected the water they returned to their village. It was getting dark as they arrived at their house. Vorn stopped by her tree. She carefully removed the stones from the roots and poured the precious water over the ground. She watched it soak into the earth and then put the stones back over the wet ground.

"I'll come back tomorrow with some more water," she told her tree.

Vorn stood looking at her tree. Suddenly she noticed something.

"Look Taan, I think there is a little bump on one of the stems," she said excitedly. "Perhaps that is the first fruit bud. The water must be helping my tree to grow."

Vorn ran into the house. "I got some water for my papaya," she said. "And I walked all the way!"

"Good," said her mother, "I know you must be tired but will you look after the baby while I prepare the meal?"

Vorn left her tin under the tap and went to play with the baby. She had forgotten all about putting the sin round her tree.

Several days later the spring in the hills dried up too. There was no water anywhere. The rain still hadn't come. Every day was hot, dry, and dusty.

"We will lose the rice crop if the rain doesn't come soon," warned Taan. "There is no point going to the field today as there is nothing we can do. Why has the rain not come?"

"I don't know," replied his mother sadly. "We have all been praying for the rains to come. Why don't you take

Vorn to look for some berries?"

"That's a good idea," said Taan, "we can eat them on the way back."

"And we can pray for the rain to come tomorrow," said Vorn, picking up her basket.

Taan and Vorn set off with their baskets to look for berries. As they passed the papaya tree Vorn looked at it. The leaves were all shrivelled up and the top of the tree hung over limply.

"My tree is dying," cried Vorn.

As Vorn looked at her dying tree, she suddenly remembered the dripping tap outside their house.

"Perhaps there is some water in my tin," said Vorn hurrying over to the tap to look.

"Yes, there is a little water in it," said Vorn, happily lifting the tin and carrying it over to her tree. She poured the last drop of water onto the roots.

"Come on!" shouted Taan who was already walking down the path. "We need to get the berries."

At last they reached the forest where the berries grew.

"I'm very tired and thirsty," said Vorn stopping by some bushes.

"I'm tired and thirsty too. Hopefully we will find lots of berries," said Taan.

"Then we can eat some," suggested Vorn.

"Not till we have picked enough to take home for the rest of the family first," said Taan.

They walked through the forest looking about for the berries. Soon Taan spotted a large bush covered with berries. Vorn couldn't help eating a few before she put some in her basket as she was so thirsty. The taste of the fresh sweet berries made her dry mouth feel good. Taan and Vorn picked the berries for some time. Vorn looked into her basket. The sight of many purple berries glistening in the basket made her feel happy. At least the family would have something nice to eat tonight.

"Perhaps the rain will come tomorrow," said Vorn hopefully.

"I hope it does rain soon," said Taan. "The rice harvest will be ruined if the rain doesn't come in the next day or two."

"I need a rest," said Vorn. "Do you think we have picked enough now? Can we eat some?"

"By the look of your face you have eaten some already!" laughed Taan, putting down his basket.

They sat down on the hard dry ground and ate some of the berries. The sky was getting dark as the sun began to set behind the hills.

"We need to go home now," said Taan, standing up.

As they came out of the forest Vorn looked up into the sky.

"Do you think there are some clouds in the sky?" said Vorn hopefully.

"I think you are just imagining it," said Taan. "It's just getting dark. Come on, Mother will be waiting for the berries."

Vorn and Taan hurried home. Their mother was very pleased to have the berries. That night the family went to bed still feeling hungry as there was no water to cook the rice and vegetables. Vorn and Taan went to bed with dirty hands and faces from picking the berries.

Vorn was very tired. It had been a long day but before she fell asleep she prayed, "Dear Father God please send the rain soon. Our rice crop will be ruined and my little papaya tree will die if the rain doesn't come. Please help us. Amen." Soon she was fast asleep.

Suddenly Vorn woke with a start. She listened carefully. Was that the sound of rain on the tin roof? She sat up and listened carefully. Yes, she was sure it was the noise of rain on the roof.

"It's raining!" she shouted out. "It's raining!"

Soon everyone was awake and running out of the house. Outside in the street all the villagers were dancing in the rain. Everyone enjoyed getting wet and thanked God that the rains had come. No one went back to bed that night but had a party. The women cooked some rice and vegetables and everyone had a great feast.

Vorn ran over to her tree. It was standing up straight. Already the rain had soaked into the ground. She knew that her tree would live now. The miracle had happened. The rain had come at last.

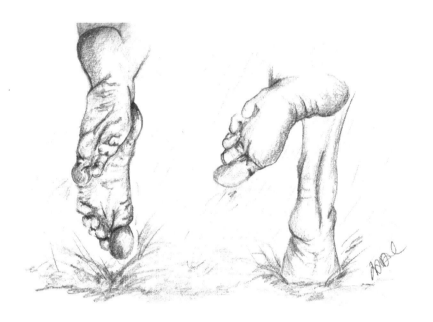

The villagers dancing in the rain

Several months later, Vorn came hurrying into the house carrying something in her hand.

"Look what I have!" she said, jumping up and down. "My tree has grown fruit."

She proudly showed the family her papaya.

"Come on everyone, we can all have a bit of my papaya."

"You certainly looked after your tree, Vorn," said her father. "Uncle Ponsee will be pleased with you when he comes to visit us next week."

"Maybe he will give Vorn another papaya tree, and then we can have more fruit next year," said Taan with a laugh.

The following week Uncle Ponsee came to visit Vorn and her family. Vorn couldn't wait to show him her tree. They all stood round looking at the tree.

"I think I will have to bring some more young trees for you to look after, Vorn," said Uncle Ponsee, looking round the small garden in front of the house. "You have plenty of room for a few more papaya trees."

"That would be great if you did. I know Vorn will take good care of them," her mother told Uncle Ponsee. She turned to Vorn and added, "And you didn't need the sin round the tree to make it produce fruit. You helped it to produce fruit by taking care of it and watering it every day."

That night Vorn dreamt about a big garden full of papaya trees and she was in charge of them all. The next morning she told her mother about her dream.

"I grew so many papayas that I gave everyone in the village some of my fruit and we never went hungry again," she announced proudly.

"I hope that dream comes true," laughed Taan.

"Yes, I think that is what I will do when I am grown up," said Vorn eating her rice. "I will sell them at the market and make so much money you won't need to spend all day in the fields."

"That dream might just come true," said her mother happily. "You know how to take care of the trees. You work hard at school. When you are a big girl you can have your own garden and grow papayas."

"And I won't put a sin round them," added Vorn. "It's God who makes trees grow, not a silly piece of cloth."

Discussion

1. What part of the story did you like best?

2. I wonder what it is like to have no rain for a long time.

3. Where would you plant a tree and what tree would it be?

4. Who would you go to, to ask about how to grow something?

5. Why is it important to keep on caring and not give up when things get difficult?

6. What do you think about "the sin" round the tree?

7. Are you superstitious about anything?

8. How do plants grow?

9. When is it important to water a tree?

10. Do you see a similarity between God and Vorn in this story? (Do you suppose God cares for us just as Vorn cared for her tree?)

11. Who can you help or care for?

12. Where is Laos? Find out about the people who live there.

The Hurricane
in Haiti

"**I HAVE JUST HAD A TEXT MESSAGE** from the Red Cross!" shouted Nessilo from inside the tent.

"What did it say?" asked his mother anxiously.

"The hurricane!" replied Nessilo in alarm as he came out of the tent. "It's due to strike here in a couple of hours. We have to evacuate the area immediately."

"It's one bad thing after another," said an old woman

standing by the next tent. "How can I leave here? Where can I go? We haven't yet recovered from the January earthquake and we are all still homeless."

"I know," replied Nessilo's mother sadly. "Our home was damaged too in the earthquake. We have nowhere to go either. What can we do?" She buried her head in her hands and wept.

"What's the matter?" asked Elisnee, seeing her mother crying. Elisnee had been to the water carrier at the far end of the camp to get fresh water to cook the evening meal.

"The hurricane is coming our way and we have to leave immediately," explained Nessilo to his sister.

"What! It's coming *our* way?" said Elisnee, putting down the bucket of water and running over to her mother.

Their friend Malik appeared running into the camp shouting: "Have you heard the news? We have to leave right away! The Red Cross says it's not safe to stay here because our tents will be blown away."

"Oh, what's going to happen to us?" cried their mother. "I can't leave here—I have to wait for your father coming back from the city."

"But you will find him there, Mother," explained Nessilo. "You can't stay here. Come on, we need to get to the city and find a safe place to stay till the hurricane has passed."

"I must stay here and keep our tent safe. It is all we have," replied their mother. "You go, Nessilo, and take your sister with you. I'll stay here and hope for the best."

"Can I come with you?" asked the old woman hopefully. "I have nowhere to go anyway, and perhaps I will find a place to stay in the city."

"Yes, of course you can come with us," replied Nessilo, grabbing some rope from the tent.

"I know a short cut through the forest to the other side of the Island," suggested Malik, pouring some water from the bucket into an empty bottle he had in his pocket.

"Will you manage to go through the forest?" Nessilo asked the old woman.

"Yes, I can walk but slowly. I don't want to keep you back," she replied.

"Don't worry, we will help you," said Elisnee taking hold of the old woman's arm.

"Can my children come along with you?" asked an anxious mother running up to the group with her two young children.

Nessilo realised this was going to be a difficult enough journey through the forest with his sister, and the added burden of an old woman. Could he cope with two young children as well? He thought about it for a moment but knew he couldn't leave them to the force of the wind if the hurricane hit their campsite. He saw the people running here and there. The whole camp was in confusion. Men were shouting instructions to the women to take their children to safety. The wind had increased in power and the tents were already flapping dangerously in the sudden gusts. The sky was dark with low black clouds and it felt very cold. Nessilo and Malik knew the danger. They had been caught in the earthquake that hit their home ten months ago and had been marooned on top of a roof for two days.

"Okay, they can come with us," Malik agreed, "but they will have to walk all the way."

"Do what the boys tell you and I will find where you are after the hurricane has passed," shouted the mother as she watched the little group set off towards the forest with her two children.

"I'll keep in touch through my mobile," Nessilo called back to his mother as they began their journey to safety.

The little group walked through the woods in silence, each carefully keeping watch where they placed their feet on the muddy path. No one wanted to slip and fall into the mud. The rain began again, falling heavily through the trees, lashing their faces and soaking their clothes. The two young children clung to the old woman's coat as they struggled behind her. Nessilo stayed at the end of the group to make sure no one got left behind. Malik was out in front leading the way with Elisnee close behind him.

"I hope these trees don't fall down in this hurricane," shouted Elisnee over the roaring sound of the wind.

"I hope so too," replied Malik, looking up at the swaying

trees above his head. "We should be at the bridge soon," he said, looking back to make sure everyone was keeping up.

Suddenly there was a loud crack followed by the sound of something smashing through the trees. Everyone stood still, not daring to move, then the crashing noise ended as suddenly as it started.

"I think whatever fell is on the ground now so it is safe to move on," said Malik, looking about him to see what had happened.

The only sound that could be heard was the wind howling through the trees and the splashing of the rain on the ground.

"Come on, the wind is getting stronger and more intense," said Malik. "We need to cross the river and go through the valley to get to the city before the hurricane strikes."

The two young children never said a word but followed the old woman closely. When they came to some fallen branches Elisnee helped the old woman over them. The children jumped onto the broken branches, then jumped off onto the other side.

"Thank goodness these two children are not giving us any bother," Nessilo thought to himself as he followed the group over the blockage on the path.

"Oh, no!" exclaimed Malik as they arrived at the river. "The bridge has been washed away by the raging river. Look, the ropes are dangling in the water."

Everyone stood looking at the torrents of water rushing along, taking branches, leaves and other debris with it. There was no way of crossing this river.

"What are we going to do now?" wailed Elisnee who up to now had been brave and excited about this adventure.

"Let's go further down the river," suggested Malik, "perhaps there is another bridge across."

"Well, we certainly can't go back," said Nessilo, "it's too late. The hurricane will hit the Island soon. Let's pray there is another bridge and that it's not down too."

"I've been praying all the way here," said a little voice from behind the old woman. "I've asked Jesus to help us get to safety."

"I'm very glad about that," laughed Nessilo, patting the

young child on her shoulder.

The tired and frightened group began to follow the river. No one knew where it would lead them but all were hoping somehow they would find a way to cross the river soon.

"Wow, look at that!" exclaimed Malik when they were stopped by a toppled tree blocking the path.

"The fallen tree is right across the river," said Elisnee in surprise.

"I guess your prayers have been answered, little one," said the old woman.

"But is it safe to cross over the river on this branch?" enquired Nessilo.

"The problem is not whether it is safe to cross," said Elisnee in alarm. "It is *how* do we cross it? I'm not walking along that tree. We will slip and fall into the river."

They all looked at the fallen tree lying across the turbulent waters below.

"It's the answer to our prayer so this must be the way to cross the river safely," said the old woman at last.

"If we sit across the tree and cling onto the trunk we can pull ourselves along it," suggested the little girl. "Before the earthquake we used to play on the trees near where we lived. Everyone tried to see who could crawl across the tree the fastest."

"Yes, but the river was shallow and you wouldn't drown if you fell off," reminded the little girl's brother.

"We can do it," said Elisnee confidently, realising the little girl had more faith than she had. "You go first to make sure it is safe, Malik."

"Here, tie this rope round your waist," suggested Nessilo handing the rope to Malik. "We will hold on to the other end just in case you do fall in."

"Good idea," said Malik tying the rope round him.

Malik went up to the fallen tree and sat across the trunk. The others all held on to the rope. Carefully he edged his way out over the open river. Little by little he made his way across the tree stopping every now and then to wipe his hands on his trousers. The bark was jaggy and sore to sit on and bits came off on his wet hands. At last he made it to the end of the tree and jumped safely onto the dry ground.

"Come on, it's safe!" he shouted over to them as he untied the rope. "But watch the branches on the trunk— they will scratch your legs and hands."

"Can you throw the rope back over?" asked Nessilo.

"You go next," said the old woman to Elisnee. "I will take the children with me. Nessilo can come behind us."

Malik wound up the rope and threw it across the river. Nessilo managed to catch it before it fell into the river. He tied it round Elisnee.

"There, that will save you if you do fall off," he assured her.

Elisnee climbed onto the tree. Her hands were shaking

and her heart pounding. She was very afraid but didn't want to show the children that she was scared to go across the tree. She also wanted to show Malik that girls are strong and brave too. Carefully she put her hands further along the trunk before moving her bottom towards her hands. Nessilo and the old woman held on to the rope. By the time she reached the middle of the river the water was covering her feet and splashing on her face. Her hands were numb with cold and she could hardly hold onto the trunk. At one point she felt herself slipping off the tree. She grabbed hold of the branch lying flat along it, afraid to move. The water swirled below her.

"Don't look down Elisnee," warned Malik from the bank of the river. "Look at me! Come on, you can make it. Sit up and move your hands forward," he instructed.

Elisnee sat up and looked at Malik who was encouraging her to move. Slowly she took one hand off the branch and placed it on the tree trunk in front of her. Then she placed the other hand further up the trunk. She moved her weight onto her hands and slid her legs along a bit. Nessilo shouted encouragement from the other side: "Go on, that's the way, easy does it. Good Elisnee, on you go – you are nearly at the end. One more big move and you're there!"

Suddenly she was in the arms of Malik who caught her as she reached the end of the tree. He lifted her from the trunk and put her safely on the ground. He untied the rope and Elisnee collapsed on the ground trembling.

"You made it," encouraged Malik. "Well done! That was a very brave thing to do all by yourself."

"Don't let go of the rope Nessilo," shouted Malik. "Keep a hold of it just in case and I will hold on at this end."

When the old woman saw that Elisnee was safely across the river, she put the little girl in front of her and the boy climbed onto the tree behind her. Nessilo followed behind the boy, tying the rope round him. Slowly they edged their way along the trunk of the tree to the other side.

"Good thing you brought that rope, Nessilo," said Malik as they all sat on the ground.

"Although we didn't need it thankfully," replied Elisnee drinking some water. "It was a lifeline wasn't it?" Everyone agreed it had helped them. They all drank some water and had a little rest.

"We must keep going," said Malik looking at his watch. "We only have an hour to get to the city before the hurricane hits us."

"Can you find out any news from your mobile?" asked Elisnee. Nessilo tried to get a signal but his mobile was dead.

"I can't get connected either," said Malik. "Maybe the network is down. I wouldn't be surprised. These destructive torrents of rain and wind could bring down the mobile masts."

Once across the river they left the forest and made their way through the valley. The mud on the road made it difficult to walk. Thick gooey mud ran down the denuded[1] hillsides stripped bare by the rain after the earthquake. The ferocious wind blew down the valley making it even more difficult to struggle against. At last they saw the city below them. No lights could be seen in the houses as darkness approached. The howling wind blew all around them as they reached the first houses of the city. Roofs had been blown off buildings and fields of crops were drowned in water; trees lay on the road and people were wading up to their waists in water carrying their few possessions above their heads.

"I don't think we will be safe here," said Elisnee, taking in the devastation in front of her. "It looks like the hurricane has reached here already. Where has all this water come from?"

"I guess it must have been the torrential rain we came through when we were in the forest," said Malik, looking for a safe path to follow.

"All the crops are wiped out," cried Elisnee who had had enough of this adventure.

Malik noticed a path high up on the hillside on the other side of the water.

"We will need to cross over to the other side and follow that path over there," he said pointing across the muddy

---

1. The hillside had no trees left on it.

water.

"Everyone hold on to each other and follow me," instructed Nessilo suddenly taking charge.

They followed others into the flood

Nessilo led the little group into the water, following others who were doing the same thing. As they waded through the raging flood they noticed some people trying to salvage whatever things they could from their homes, while radios, beds, chairs and food floated past them in the filthy, muddy water washed down from the hills. They reached the other side safely and followed the path down to the city.

Eventually they reached the city streets which were also covered with water.

"There's shelter in the church at the top of the hill over there!" shouted a man as the tired, wet group made their way through the flooded streets.

"Come on, we'll be safe in the church," said Malik, happily taking the old woman's arm and helping her up the hill to the church. Many other people were rushing to the safety of higher ground. Inside the dark church Nessilo groped his way to a pew and sat down exhausted. The others followed. The old woman took the soaking clothes off the children before removing her wet coat. They spread out their wet clothes over the pews. Suddenly a light filled the dark church. One by one candles were lit and soon the whole church was bright with the effect of hundreds of shimmering flames. A choir began to sing and all the people joined in. Later on as the candles burned out, the church became quiet.

"Hopefully the network will be fixed by tomorrow and we can contact our families again," whispered Nessilo as he tried to get comfortable on the hard pew.

"As we were coming into the church a man told me that the road to the capital has been washed away and the city is cut off because many of the bridges have been taken out too," said Malik. "At least we made it here before the hurricane struck."

"Yes, I think there will be a lot of destruction caused by this hurricane," replied Nessilo. "Did you see the damaged houses we passed?"

"Did you notice all the wasted food, ruined by the flood water?" said Elisnee sleepily.

"What speed does the wind get up to when it is a hurricane?" asked the young boy who felt better now that they were safe.

"It can be as much as much as 155 miles per hour at the peak," replied Malik.

"Try to sleep," the old woman told the children as they curled up on the pew.

"I will thank God for getting us safely here and answering our prayer for a way across the river," said the little girl as she put her head on the old woman's knee.

Soon everyone in the church was quiet, tired out from the events of the day. The hurricane could be heard howling round the roof of the church outside. Inside, the small group of people who had struggled through the forest, across the raging river and down the valley to safety, were thankfully able to sleep.

The hurricane only lasted a couple of hours before blowing on to the mainland. Everyone stayed where they were for the night and in the morning the blue helmets of the UN peace-keeping force could be seen in the streets. Food was brought to the cut-off city by helicopter and distributed among the people in the church. Warm blankets were given to those who needed them. Soon the telephone lines and the mobile networks were back up and working, the electric supply reconnected and fresh drinking water supplied to everyone.

The old woman thanked Malik and Nessilo.

"Where are you going now?" asked Elisnee as the old woman said goodbye.

"Oh, I will find somewhere to live here in the city," said the old woman. "I lost my home and family in the January earthquake and have been wandering about for ten months. Now I want to settle down. Perhaps I will help here in the church." The old woman smiled as she walked away.

Nessilo was at last able to get a signal on his mobile. "I've got through to our mother, Elisnee," said Nessilo happily. "I was able to get connected. Mother says Father is safe too. He made it back to the campsite, but was afraid we had been swept away. Some of the tents are torn and some were blown away, but we can fix that. We have to stay here till Father comes for us." Nessilo was able to reassure the two young children, who had accompanied them on their journey, that their mother was safe too. "You two will come back to the refugee camp with us," he said. "Your mother is waiting for you there."

"What will you do, Malik?" asked Elisnee as she realised their adventure together was over.

"I will stay here in the city for a while to help with the clearing up. I will come to the camp next week to see how you are getting on," said Malik. "Hopefully we will all be re-housed soon."

"Well, I'm glad you came and helped us to safety," she said with a smile, "even if it was a bit scary."

Elisnee turned to the two young children. She took their hands saying, "And thank you for praying for us. Without your help we may not have got here."

"It was not us who got you safely here, but God," the little girl smiled.

"Quite right," said Elisnee as they all went off to find something to eat.

Discussion

1. Imagine a hurricane was about to come to your country. How would you feel?

2. Have you ever been in a difficult situation?

3. When have you been afraid?

4. Do you think God helped Malik and Nessilo, the old woman and the two children? How?

5. What part of the story did you like?

6. Which part did you not like?

7. Who helped when the hurricane came?

8. What can you do to help when other countries are experiencing a disaster?

9. Why do we have disasters?

10. How does a hurricane happen?

11. Where is Haiti?

12. Find out what other countries have hurricanes.

Fire in the Highlands of Scotland

IN A VALLEY far away in the Highlands of Scotland, before there was electricity, there was a shepherd's cottage surrounded by mountains. Kenneth, aged 8 years, lived there with his mother, father, brother Sandy and two sisters Maggie and Lisa. His father looked after the sheep that grazed on the hillside. Several months after the ewes had their lambs they were gathered together and taken down to the fank[2] to be sheared.

It was just an ordinary day in the cottage. Kenneth was peeling the potatoes; his mother, sitting by the fireside, was darning some socks and the toddler Lisa was playing at her feet. His father was busy shearing the sheep with the other shepherds at the fank three miles away.

---

2. *A wooden or stone pen for keeping the sheep in.*

Looking up from her darning, mother asked, "Sandy, have you not changed out of your school clothes yet?" Sandy had just started school and he didn't want to take off his new school trousers and shirt.

"Can't I keep my new trousers on a little longer?" pleaded Sandy. "I want to show Father and the other shepherds my new school clothes."

"No, you will get them dirty," replied his mother. "Your teacher will not be pleased with you if you go to school with your new trousers in a mess."

Sandy went through to the bedroom to change his clothes. Mother finished her darning while Kenneth emptied the potato peelings into the bucket beside the sink.

"Here Maggie, take these socks to our room and put

them in your father's drawer," said their mother, folding the socks into a ball. "Kenneth, you can take the peelings out to the hens while I start cooking the dinner. The men will be coming up from the fank soon and they will be hungry for their meal."

Maggie took the socks and went out of the room.

"I can't get through the corridor!" yelled Maggie from the doorway. "There's smoke everywhere."

Kenneth and their mother rushed to the door. Smoke filled the corridor pouring into the room when the door was opened.

"Maggie, run and get your father and the other shepherds!" shouted their mother as she ran back into the kitchen, coughing badly. She picked up Lisa who was standing by the fire crying and ran out of the house.

Seeing the smoke filling the kitchen Kenneth immediately emptied the potato peelings into the sink and filled the bucket with water. He ran to the open bedroom door and threw the water onto the flames that were now licking up the wall and over the ceiling.

Kenneth rushed back to the sink and filled the bucket again. The flames were getting higher. He could hear the roar as the fire took hold. Back and forth he ran with buckets of water. Still the flames burned inside the room. The smoke filled the corridor making it difficult for Kenneth to breathe. Then the tap ran dry! Quick as a flash Kenneth ran to the burn[3] nearby. He jumped into the burn and filled up his bucket with water. The water spilled out as he ran back to the house. Smoke was billowing out of the front door now, making it impossible to get back into the house.

Kenneth then ran round to the back of the house and threw the water through the broken window. He didn't wait to see how bad the fire was but continued to run to the burn, fill up the bucket and throw the water into the blazing room. The varnished wood just kept on burning.

At last, over half an hour later, the Land Rover arrived at

3. *Small river.*

the shepherd's cottage. Their father, Maggie and the other shepherds jumped out. By that time, however, the flames had been extinguished. Kenneth had put out the fire single handed!

"Be careful going into the house!" warned Dougie, one of the shepherds, as their father rushed towards the door.

"I can't find Sandy!" screamed their mother frantically. She had been running about looking for her son, shouting and screaming. Lisa was standing quite still in the middle of the path crying. She was too afraid to move. Maggie ran up to her, picked her up and cuddled her. Two of the shepherds helped to look for Sandy while Dougie went into the house after their father.

"Oh no, I can feel something hard," cried their father as he felt inside the burned out wardrobe. He pulled something out, thinking it was Sandy. Thankfully it was just an old battered suitcase wrapped in a blanket.

"What a mess," said Dougie looking round the gutted room. Everything was ruined. Clothes lay in a heap of burnt material. The walls and ceiling were covered in thick black soot. The broken window was black with the smoke. Water covered the floor. The wardrobe was a charred box.

"Fire can do a lot of damage," added Dougie. Father rushed from room to room shouting for Sandy.

"He's not in here, thank goodness," said their father once he realised that the boy was not in the house.

"He must have escaped through the door when the fire started," said Dougie as they came out of the smouldering house.

"Oh, where can he be?" cried their mother, still searching for Sandy.

As the men stood in the yard trying to work out where to look next, a voice came from the garage which was just across from the house.

"It's okay, he's over here!" called out one of the searchers.

Everyone ran into the big garage.

There, hiding behind the huge tractor wheel, was a very frightened Sandy. Mother rushed over to him, pulled him from behind the wheel and hugged him tightly.

"We thought you were in the fire," she cried. "We thought we had lost you."

Sandy stood beside his mother crying. "I didn't mean to drop the match, I didn't mean to! It burnt my fingers," he stammered.

"What were you doing with a match?" asked Dougie.

"I couldn't see my old trousers in the wardrobe," Sandy replied with a sniff. "So I struck a match and looked into the wardrobe. Then the match burnt my fingers so I dropped it. Then I ran away."

Nobody spoke as they moved out of the garage and down the road to the bothy.[4] In the bothy Dougie and the other shepherds made a pot of tea and some sandwiches before going back to their own cottages.

However, no-one felt like eating that night. They sat and stared at the plate of sandwiches too upset to eat. The ghillies[5] returned from a day out hunting and were told about the fire.

"The children had better sleep here with you tonight," said their father. "The house is too smoky for them." Then turning to the children he added, "You will be fine staying here with the ghillies."

Exhausted, afraid and sad at the loss of their home, the children went to bed in the bothy. A very sombre group tried to sleep that night.

---

4. *A building used by the ghillies to sleep in when on a hunting expedition.*
5. *Ghillie or gillie is a Scots term that refers to a man or a boy who acts as an attendant who helps a group of hunters to find the deer.*

Mother and Father decided to stay in the house despite the smell of smoke just in case anything happened. In the middle of the night Father heard a crackling sound. Afraid that the smouldering timbers might have caught alight again he jumped out of bed and began pulling down the beams in the ceiling.

The next morning a subdued family drank big mugs of tea as they wondered what to do next. No-one had slept that night. And no-one had thought to praise Kenneth for putting out the fire. Everyone had been so concerned about Sandy and happy that he was found safe and unharmed that they forgot all about poor Kenneth who was afraid of fire for many years to come.

Although this was a small house fire in a quiet area, it affected the people involved just as much as if it had been a big forest fire in an important part of the world.

Discussion

1. What part of the story did you like best and what part did you not like?

2. Why did you not like that part?

3. How do you think Kenneth managed to put out the fire single handed?

4. Do you think God helped him even though he didn't ask God for help?

5. Have you ever been afraid?

6. Would you have been angry with Sandy for starting the fire?

7. What would you have given Kenneth for putting out the fire all by himself?

8. Who would you like to be, Sandy or Kenneth? Why?

9. How would you feel if you had been Kenneth when no-one praised or thanked him?

10. Where is God when danger strikes?

11. When is a fire a good thing and when is it bad?

12. Where is Scotland? Find out about the people who live there.